Bloodred Sky

by
Anne Schraff

Perfection Learning Corporation
Logan, Iowa 51546-0500

Cover Illustration: Carlotta A. Tormey

© 2003 Perfection Learning Corporation.
All rights reserved. No part of this book may be
reproduced, stored in a retrieval system, or
transmitted in any form or by any means, electronic,
mechanical, photocopying, recording, or otherwise,
without prior permission of the publisher.

For information, contact:
Perfection Learning Corporation
1000 North Second Avenue, P.O. Box 500,
Logan, Iowa 51546-0500.
Tel: 1-800-831-4190 • Fax: 1-800-543-2745

Paperback ISBN 0-7891-5903-1
Cover Craft® ISBN 0-7569-1176-1
perfectionlearning.com
Printed in the U.S.A.

1 2 3 4 5 6 PP 07 06 05 04 03 02

1

Seven months ago, Jesse Garcia and his crewmates left Earth. Now, within minutes, they would be on the surface of Mars. The five young men and women had been chosen by the Mars Exploration Committee (MEC). They were to join the small Martian colony that had been established five years earlier.

When 25-year-old Jesse found out he was one of the committee's choices, he had been filled with awe and excitement. Since he was a small boy, Jesse had spent many hours peering at the strange red planet through a telescope. He grew up hearing all the crazy tales about Mars and Martians. Never in his wildest imagination, though, had he thought he would actually spend a year on Mars. But now it was happening.

"Just think," Robin Palmer said as she strapped herself into the landing module. "The pink Martian sky and the red Martian soil will soon be home to us." Robin was one of Jesse's crewmates. The 24-year-old had been chosen because of her knowledge of agriculture. She was to help develop a large terrarium for growing edible plants on Mars. All the food eaten by the colonists now was transported from an orbiting space station. This was an expensive process. Once the terrarium was finished, the colony could raise its own fruits and vegetables.

"Yeah, it's going to be just like home, all right," quipped Alex Osgood, settling in beside her. "*If* you don't mind the freezing temperatures and the raging windstorms. Not to mention the total lack of all forms of life. Oh, and don't forget, if you stick your head out without oxygen and protective gear, the radiation will fry your brains *while* you're choking to death. Yep, good old Mars. Soon to be home sweet home."

Alex Osgood was an engineer. He was in charge of the landing module the crew would use to leave the spaceship once they landed on the planet. Alex was about 27, glib, and sometimes annoying. Jesse didn't like him very much because he always seemed to dwell on the negative. Alex was constantly reminding the crew of the misfortunes that could overtake them in the months ahead. But now Jesse smiled at Alex's remarks. He knew that beneath the jokes lurked a sense of uneasiness. Only days earlier a frightening event had occurred on Mars. Elliott Gaines, one of the colonists, had been out in his Mars Rover when he disappeared on the Utopian Plains. A search party found his Rover undamaged, but there was no sign of Gaines.

The crew members on Jesse's ship had been asking one another what had happened. What procedure did Gaines slip up on? they wondered. Where had he gone? Did his oxygen mask fail, causing him to become confused? If so, did he then fall into a crevice and die? But still, where was the body? The colonists had searched everywhere between the Rover and the colony. Surely they had examined all crevices in the area. But no trace of Gaines had been found.

As the safety engineer, Jesse knew he would be expected to investigate the mishap. Now, as he prepared to land, he wondered what he'd find—if anything.

The spaceship that the crew of five was traveling in was longer than a football field. But after seven months, most of them had some form of cabin fever. Many felt a burning desire to get out of the ship and just walk around in the open. Even if it was in a strange and hostile environment like Mars. They were anxious to get to their new workstations, so this final stage of the journey was welcomed. All quickly climbed into the landing module and waited as Alex skillfully set it down onto the surface of the planet. Once there, they watched as the spaceship they had come on turned and began its long journey back to Earth.

Jesse knew what to expect when they reached the colony. He had seen many photographs of the settlement while he was still training on Earth. Each colonist would live in an apartment-sized aluminum building, linked by an underground walkway. Each building had a bedroom, living room, kitchen, and bathroom. No windows, of course, because all buildings in the settlement were buried underground. The only exception was the moundlike observatory. It had a clear roof that blocked the harmful radiation of the sun. Eleven feet of soil protected the other buildings.

As the landing module opened for the crew members to leave, Jesse gasped, "Man, the soil really *is* red. And so is the sky. Almost bloodred! This is amazing!"

"Look at the huge mountains in the distance," Robin said. "They're beautiful."

"Don't get carried away," Steve Saunders, another engineer, said. "I've been here before, and believe me, it gets old real fast. There's nowhere to go for pizza, no theaters, no shopping malls. Nothing."

The last of the five new crew members was Bianca Forest, an expert in animal breeding. With her help, small livestock would eventually be introduced into the settlement to create a permanent protein supply.

"Just imagine when we get the terrarium built," Robin said, gazing around. "It'll have big, dome-shaped structures with fruit trees and gardens. It'll have ponds for fish and areas for raising chickens and rabbits. People will stroll around, just like on Earth. Then Mars will *really* feel like a second home."

"Maybe for you," Alex laughed. "But not for me. I'm serving my year, and then I'm out of here. I want the real thing—not an imitation."

Jesse glanced up. The spaceship that had brought them was now only a glowing silver disk in the Martian sky. Jesse felt a twinge of misgiving to see their only means of getting off the planet vanishing. A commitment to Mars wasn't like signing up for a weekend rafting trip on the Colorado River, he reminded himself. If he didn't like the rafting trip, he could always go home.

Jesse glanced across the Martian plain. In the distance, he could see several large Mars Rovers approaching. The big vehicles were built like tractors, with large tires and antennae. To Jesse, they looked like big bugs. A few minutes later, the Rover rolled up to take the new colonists to the settlement.

The original construction of all the apartments and utility areas had been an awesome and expensive project. But the seeds of a real community existed on Mars. Ten scientists, engineers, and other skilled people already lived there. And now, with Jesse's group, there would be 15.

"A population explosion," Alex had joked on the trip there.

When they arrived at the settlement, the new colonists were taken to their apartments.

Jesse was content with his new living quarters. They seemed comfortable enough. Nothing luxurious, but he had a nice bed, a recliner, a couple of roomy closets, and a computer nook. The computers, along with all the other electronic devices in the colony, were operated by a huge generator, deep in the core of the settlement.

Jesse spent a few minutes getting settled. As he was putting away the last of his things, Robin poked her head into the room. She had slipped into jeans and a T-shirt and had a smile on her face.

"I really like my quarters!" she beamed. "When I get my pictures up, it'll be perfect. You know, Jesse, this is just like a little city down here. I could forget I'm even on Mars."

"Yeah," Jesse agreed. "It's not too bad."

It was just like Robin to be enthusiastic—even about an underground bunker. Jesse had gotten to know Robin quite well on the seven-month journey to Mars. He liked her very much. She was fresh and funny and sweet. Her high spirits helped everyone on the flight from Earth. When the crew members got cranky or depressed, Robin was able to kid them all back into a good mood.

Suddenly, a voice came over the public address system.

Dr. Chin requests that all colonists report to the observatory in five minutes for a short meeting. I repeat: All colonists should report to the observatory in five minutes.

Robert Chin, the commander of the colony, was a 40-year-old Chinese American engineer. He was from Los Angeles and was a longtime member of the space program.

"Guess that's us," Robin said.

"Yeah, let's go," Jesse replied.

A few minutes later, all 15 of the colonists were gathered in the observatory. Dr. Chin began by welcoming the five new members.

"Welcome to MEC II," he said. "We are happy to have five bright new faces among us. Robin Palmer and Bianca Forest are here to help develop the terrarium that will house plants and livestock. Engineers Alex Osgood and Steve Saunders will help us with our technical programs. And Jesse Garcia will oversee the safety procedures."

A general murmur of welcome came from the original colonists.

"As you all know, we have a very important job here on Mars," the commander continued. "Our goal is to explore the possibilities of terraforming the planet, making it suitable for human life. So far I've been very pleased with the efforts and enthusiasm of the first group. I'm sure you new members will be equally productive. And I'm sure you're eager to see your new workstations. I've assigned five of our original members to take you there. Any questions before we break up?"

"I have a question," Jimmy Manning, a scientist, said. "Has there been any progress in finding out what happened to Elliott Gaines?"

Instantly, the comment cast a shadow over the cheerful nature of the welcome.

Jesse looked at Dr. Chin, who was obviously saddened at the mention of the lost colonist.

"Not as yet," Dr. Chin said. "We hope that as safety engineer, Mr. Garcia will be able to shed some light on what happened. There had to be some flaw or error in this tragic incident. And we want to make sure it never happens again." He looked at Jesse then. "Garcia, after checking out your workstation, please report to my quarters."

"Yes, sir," Jesse replied.

An hour later, Jesse arrived at the commander's door.

"You wanted to see me?" Jesse asked.

"Yes," Dr. Chin replied in a serious tone as he ushered Jesse in. "No doubt you know about Elliott Gaines?"

"Yes, sir," Jesse replied. "We were radioed with the news just a few days before arriving here."

"Good," Dr. Chin replied. "Then you realize that you must leave no stone unturned in your probe of his disappearance. It has caused enormous distress in our small community. And it has caused morale to deteriorate. We are so few that the loss of one is felt by all."

"Of course," Jesse replied. "Do you have any theories about what might have happened?"

"Undoubtedly one of the safety systems failed," the commander replied. "Perhaps his oxygen system malfunctioned or the temperature monitor in his suit failed."

"Either sounds possible," Jesse agreed.

"Yes, but where is the body?" Dr. Chin asked, obviously puzzled and upset. "That is the haunting question. If it were simply a malfunction, there should be a body . . ."

"Could he have fallen into a crevice?" Jesse asked.

"There are no crevices in that area large enough to conceal a body," Dr. Chin replied. "But—who knows?"

"I'll go out in the Rover tomorrow and examine the exact spot where Gaines vanished," Jesse said. "Maybe I'll notice something that's been overlooked."

"Good," Dr. Chin said. "We need a fresh viewpoint on the incident." The pained expression deepened on the man's face, and he reached out and seized Jesse's arm. "You know, there are great psychological challenges for humans living in an environment such as this. The isolation, the sense of distance from home and loved ones. When a tragic mystery such as this occurs, it can easily give rise to uncertainty and rumors. Sometimes very bizarre rumors."

"Such as?" Jesse asked.

"Well, there are always moments of dissension among people living in such close quarters as these," Dr. Chin said. "There are bound to be. Elliott was a good scientist, but he had his oddities, as we all do. There are ugly whispers that another colonist may have had a hand in his disappearance. Someone who had quarreled with him in the past or had a difference of opinion. That is, of course, ridiculous. But, you see, in the absence of concrete facts, frightening scenarios tend to take root."

"Well, we'll find out soon enough," Jesse said. "Tomorrow I'll take a Rover to the exact location of the disappearance. Will you accompany me, sir?"

"Absolutely," the commander said. "I'll do anything I can to help."

"Until this mystery is solved, I'll make it my number one priority," Jesse promised.

"Excellent, Garcia," Dr. Chin said, walking Jesse to the door. "We're all depending on you to do just that."

2

Early the next morning, Jesse and Dr. Chin suited up and left the colony in a Mars Rover. They drove to the location where Gaines's vehicle had been found by the earlier search party. They made their way to the exact spot, which was noted by large Xs painted on rocks. Due to the low force of gravity, the two men could not walk normally. Instead, they made high, springing steps as they moved along. Jesse was delighted by the sensation the bouncing steps gave him. It was like being on a gigantic trampoline.

"Right here," Dr. Chin said. "This is the spot where we found the Rover."

"Were there any signs of a struggle in the area?" Jesse asked.

Dr. Chin looked troubled again. "A struggle? No, there was no sign of a struggle."

Jesse nodded and began inspecting the area. As he did, he was reminded of a radio program that a local station had played every Halloween when he was small. It was a dramatization of *The War of the Worlds*, a science fiction story by H. G. Wells. The narrator described horrible bug-eyed, lipless Martians attacking desperate policemen and soldiers. When the play was first broadcast back in 1938, it was not introduced as a play. Listeners believed Martians were really invading Earth. Frightened people drove their cars madly away from the city. When Jesse first heard the play, he knew it was make-believe, but he had been scared anyway because he was a kid.

Now, as he inspected the area, he wondered if there *were* life forms on Mars and if maybe one of them had grabbed Elliott and dragged him away. Then Jesse smiled because, of course, such an idea was ridiculous. Some form of life may have existed on Mars millions of years ago when there was water on the planet. But even then it was probably just one-celled creatures. Certainly no bug-eyed, lipless monsters!

Suddenly, Dr. Chin came up alongside Jesse and grasped the sleeve of his suit. He spoke in a soft voice as if somebody might be listening, even though they were absolutely alone.

"Jesse, I was not going to tell you this, it's so ridiculous," the commander said. "But I've decided it's important that you know everything as you proceed with your investigation. One of our colonists, Dr. Lara Soto, raised the possibility of intelligent creatures on this planet who might have kidnapped Elliott Gaines. Dr. Soto is a highly educated scientist, which made her theory all the more frightening."

Jesse chuckled. "That's weird, all right," he said.

"Of course it is," Dr. Chin said, still gripping Jesse's sleeve. "You see, Dr. Soto was quite upset when Gaines vanished. I believe there was a . . . a personal relationship between the two of them. Anyway, she came out here on her own and searched. And she claims to have found strange tracks in the soil. Tracks that resemble the footprints of *birds*, of all things!"

BLOODRED SKY

"Birds?" Jesse asked in surprise. "But there's no life on Mars. Certainly no birds!"

"I know, I know," Dr. Chin said. "I am sure it was just the wind that blew the soil into strange drifts. This formed certain patterns that Dr. Soto mistook for enormous bird tracks."

"That would explain it," Jesse replied. He wondered how an intelligent scientist like Dr. Soto could ever believe such a theory.

An hour later, the two men decided to return to the settlement. "I've examined the entire area," Jesse told Dr. Chin. "I don't see anything out of the ordinary."

"Nor do I," the commander replied. "We might as well go back. It's almost lunchtime."

On the way back to the colony, Jesse thought about Lara Soto. He remembered meeting her in the observatory the day before. She had greeted him and his four crewmates politely enough. But Jesse realized now that she had been more withdrawn than the others. As if she trusted no one.

Jesse glanced around at the bleak, red landscape that stretched as far as he could see. Not a tree or shrub in sight. Not even a weed. He wondered again how anyone could possibly believe that life existed in this barren place.

At lunch, Jesse looked around for Dr. Soto. He saw her sitting alone at a table across the room. The tray of food in front of her remained untouched.

Dr. Chin saw him looking at her and said softly, "Dr. Lara Soto. She is the scientist who found the so-called bird tracks."

"Does she have any proof of the tracks?" Jesse asked.

"Yes, she photographed them," Chin replied. "The images were interesting, of course, but surely the work of the wind. But Lara has been adamant about her theory. She's come to me several times insisting that the bird tracks are significant to the disappearance of Gaines."

Jesse shook his head. "Some people just refuse to accept the obvious," he said.

Jesse had read all the fantastic literature about Mars. As early as 1894, scientists such as the famous Percival Lowell wrote about life on the planet. He claimed that the Martians were more intelligent than humans and that they had invented marvelous gadgets that humans had never even thought of. More recently, scientists believed they had spotted water canals on Mars. The presence of the canals proved to them that there was intelligent life on the planet. But later investigation disproved all theories. Mars could not support life because the atmosphere was too thin and the temperatures too low.

The planet had not always been that way, however. Scientists now knew for a fact that Mars once had a wet and warm climate. Valleys and dried lake beds indicate where water had once flowed and accumulated. The size of the valleys indicates that very large amounts of water, maybe even an ocean, once covered the surface. But that was millions of years ago. Mars was now a desert planet without water, with bitter-cold, windy plains and towering, lifeless mountains.

After finishing his lunch, Jesse mingled with the other colonists. He wanted to find clues of any trouble among them that might have led to Gaines's disappearance. Perhaps one of them had slipped up on a safety procedure he or she was responsible for and had accidentally caused Gaines's death. Perhaps to cover the mistake, he or she had disposed of his body in some remote canyon, far away from the place where his Rover had been found. Anything was possible.

As Jesse was making conversation with another colonist, Lara Soto walked up and interrupted. "Excuse me. You're Jesse Garcia, the safety engineer, right?"

"Yes, and you're Dr. Lara Soto," Jesse said, smiling. She was a very beautiful woman with smooth dark skin and lively eyes. "I understand you're working on long-range ideas for making this planet livable."

"Oh yes. We have great plans," Lara said. "Not tiny underground apartments. We don't want to live here like rats forever. We hope for a kind of sheltered atmosphere where we can live as we do on Earth." She reached out then and gently touched Jesse's arm. "I desperately need to talk to you in private. Is that possible?" she asked.

"Sure," Jesse said. "Why don't we sit over there?" He motioned to a corner of the room where a great artificial potted palm shielded one of the tables.

"That's fine," Dr. Soto said. She followed him across the room. They sat at the table, across from each other.

"Please call me Lara," she began.

"And call me Jesse," Jesse said.

"All right, Jesse. You're conducting an investigation into the disappearance of Elliott Gaines, right?" Lara asked.

"Yes," Jesse replied. "I'm going over all the safety procedures of the colony in general. And I'm investigating Gaines's disappearance in particular. What can you tell me about him?"

Lara shook her head sadly. "He was a genius," she said. "A brilliant man. He had plans for something called Worldcity. A clear roof would cover a vast area of Mars, and beneath that roof people could live ordinary lives. Jogging, riding bikes, attending concerts. Elliott had such wonderful plans, and we were working together on them. His loss is both professionally and personally shattering to me."

"I can imagine," Jesse said.

The young woman looked directly into Jesse's eyes. "Elliott was a very cautious man," she said. "He would *never* have left the Rover and gone wandering off. He was not one to take risks. Elliott was a logical, conscientious person who went by the book. That is why I know that some other force took him."

"What exactly do you think happened?" Jesse asked.

Lara hesitated. She studied Jesse's face as if trying to decide if he was the sort of person who would give a bizarre theory a fair hearing. At last she continued. "Could you meet me at my apartment this afternoon? I want to show you something to do with Elliott's disappearance."

"Yes, of course," Jesse said. "I'd like to talk to a few more people here. Then I'll come."

"Good. I'll see you later then," Lara

said, standing up. Then she walked away.

As he watched her leave the room, Jesse wasn't sure what to make of the intense young woman. He knew she was intelligent. Only those with very high IQs were chosen for the MEC II project. They also had to be physically strong and mentally tough. Dr. Chin had implied that Lara Soto's mind was unstable, but Jesse had a hard time believing that. She seemed so reasonable. Still, nothing was impossible. The workings of the human mind were hard to nail down. Jesse had once heard that no person is completely sane or completely insane. All humans, under certain stresses, were capable of going off the deep end.

Jesse began wandering around the room again, talking to some of the original MEC crew. As far as he could tell, nothing out of the ordinary had occurred between any of them and Elliott Gaines. Gaines was respected by the others, though some of them thought him to be a little odd. But Jesse detected no animosity among those he spoke to and certainly nothing that would explain Gaines's mysterious disappearance.

After about a half hour, he headed toward Lara Soto's apartment. When he knocked on the door, she responded immediately.

"Come in," she said. "And thank you for coming. Please, have a seat over there." She motioned to a sofa, where Jesse sat down. On the coffee table in front of the sofa was a stack of photographs.

Lara sat beside him. "Look at these," she said, handing him the stack.

Jesse looked at what first seemed to be photographs of Martian soil, the red dirt. But then he made out patterns. The odd-shaped tracks looked like a supersonic airliner flying backward. The wings, instead of being swept slightly back, were thrust forward. Both the tail and the nose of the plane were long and thin.

Jesse looked at all the pictures, one after another. Some were close-ups, some more distant shots. In the last picture, the odd-shaped tracks were close to the tires of a Rover. He looked up at Dr. Soto. "Is this one of the tires of Elliott Gaines's Rover?" he asked.

"Yes," she answered.

BLOODRED SKY

"So these tracklike patterns seem to be approaching the Rover, and others are going away. Is that right?" Jesse asked.

"Exactly," Lara replied.

"The tracks look pretty big," Jesse said.

"They're 12 inches long from the middle toe to the end of the hind toe," Lara said. She hurried to her desk and brought out a diagram. She had drawn the tracks, and now she pointed to the various features.

"Here, the forward line, is the middle toe. Here, the line leading out the rear is the hind toe. And these two are the outer toes," she said, as if she were teaching a class in anatomy.

Jesse felt the room growing uncomfortably warm although the temperature was perfectly controlled and unchanging. He was getting nervous, but he didn't want to show it. "So, Lara . . . what are you telling me?" he asked hesitantly.

"These are the tracks of a large bird," Lara said. "There is no doubt of that. The tracks are similar to those of herons found on Earth. Not exactly the same, but similar. The tracks lead to the Mars Rover

Elliott was driving when he disappeared, and then they lead away. You'll note that the imprints leading away are deeper. As if the creature was heavier. As if it . . . carried a burden."

Jesse was struggling with the hilarious image that was forming in his mind. A giant, long-legged heron carrying away a full-sized man. He didn't want to crack a smile for fear of offending Dr. Soto. But it was all he could do to keep a serious expression on his face. He took a deep breath in an attempt to regain his composure.

"So then, you think some kind of . . . bird had something to do with the disappearance of Elliott Gaines?" he finally asked.

"Inwardly, you are laughing at me, aren't you?" Lara demanded. "Don't apologize. Dr. Chin believes I'm crazy too. I overheard him talking to another colonist and saying the living conditions on Mars could cause some to have mental breakdowns. He thinks I'm one of them. But these tracks I photographed are real, Jesse. You cannot deny what's been captured on film!"

"Lara, I don't mean to laugh at you," Jesse said. "I'm just trying to understand this. Can we agree that there are no living creatures on Mars, like animals or fish or . . . birds? I mean, we've known for a long time that this is a dead planet, right?"

"We've *thought* for a long time that this is a dead planet," Lara corrected him. "Obviously, I have evidence to the contrary. I know it sounds crazy, Jesse, but I cannot dismiss this evidence." She shook her head and continued. "No, I cannot agree that there are no living things on this planet beyond us. The evidence is to the contrary."

"But, decades ago, back in the 1990s, it was absolutely established that Mars cannot support life as we know it," Jesse pressed. "Eons ago, the atmosphere was different on Mars, but now it can't possibly support life. Lara, you can't seriously believe that there are giant Martian birds flying around."

"I don't know *what* I believe," Lara said. "And I don't know for sure what those tracks are. But I *do* know they are real.

Maybe the tracks were made by a human being, one of the other colonists, for example. I have no idea why someone would do such a thing. All I know is these are bird tracks or replicas of bird tracks. And they lead to and from Elliott's Rover. I'm sure they have *something* to do with his disappearance!"

"Well, I'm here to look into what happened to Gaines," Jesse said. "I promise I won't ignore any evidence, no matter how strange, until I get to the bottom of this."

Lara looked down at her hands then. "Thank you, Jesse. As you can imagine, I . . . have no real friends in the colony anymore."

As Jesse looked at the young woman next to him, lectures from his college psychology classes went through his mind. *Paranoia. Feelings of isolation. The belief that no one likes you or that everyone is out to get you.*

"I doubt that you have no friends, Lara," he said. "Most of the others realize what a loss you've experienced. They probably just don't know what to say to you." His words were meant to comfort her, but he knew they were meaningless. He really didn't know the situation here. He hadn't been in the settlement long enough.

"I haven't gotten to know the new colonists yet, except for you, Jesse," Lara said. "Maybe they'll be different. But the ones already here think I'm crazy. They thought Elliott was crazy too. The general opinion is that he got out of the Rover and simply wandered into the wilderness. They say he just snapped. According to some of them, Elliott probably kept going until he dropped of exhaustion and died. They think his remains are lying at the bottom of some crevice."

Jesse considered that theory. Could it be that Elliott *had* simply snapped? From firsthand experience, Jesse knew how hard it was to spend months in space. There were times when he had longed to drive to the local fast-food joint for a cheeseburger and fries. At times he had yearned to see a blue sky and the ridge of green mountains that rose behind his home in Redwood City, California. He had been on Mars for less than 48 hours, and yet he had already thought of home several times. Gaines had been here for five years! Earth must have seemed so far away to him. At times, he must have felt so isolated, so lonely. It was no wonder he snapped—if that's what had happened.

3

The next morning, Jesse returned to the location where Elliott Gaines had vanished. This time he took Robin Palmer with him. Jesse wanted to examine the area again. And Robin was searching for the best possible site for the terrarium. She could hardly contain her enthusiasm for the project as they drove.

"See," Robin explained, "as the population of the colony grows, there'll be a need for a steady food supply. Hundreds, even thousands, of colonists cannot be dependent on food brought in from a space station. We'll need to be self-sufficient. And that's just what the terrarium will allow us to be."

"You're really jazzed by all this, aren't you?" Jesse asked with a smile.

During the long journey, Robin had been the most cheerful of the team members. It seemed she never had a bad day. She never got irritable or bored. She had told Jesse that she was both thrilled and honored to be part of the MEC II team.

"Yeah, I guess I am jazzed," Robin admitted, smiling. "Aren't you, Jesse? We're part of something really awesome. We're like the explorers I used to read about in my history books—Christopher Columbus, Magellan, Lewis and Clark. Discovering the frontier—new lands, new routes, new people. Only we're discovering a planet, Jesse! We're actually moving the frontier to space!"

The Rover moved slowly over the uneven terrain, dodging the larger rocks. The Utopian Plains were generally flat. But there were large depressions here or there where meteors had struck.

"Yeah, it's exciting, all right," Jesse admitted. "My buddies from college are all fired up about laying the plans for new freeways or building new skyscrapers. Me? I'm on Mars! Either I'm the luckiest guy in the world to be chosen for this job, or I'm a fool for wanting to be here. I haven't decided which. But, seriously, Robin. Do you really think that someday thousands of humans will live here?"

BLOODRED SKY 33

"Absolutely," Robin declared. "I was talking to Dr. Soto last night. She told me that the apartment towers that are being planned could house half a million people. Just imagine!"

"Pretty incredible," Jesse agreed. But he knew he wouldn't be here by the time that happened. He was proud of being part of MEC II, but he didn't want to spend more than a year here. Seven months coming and seven going, added to the year, meant 26 months away from Earth. That was about as big a chunk of his life as he was willing to give to the Martian project.

"This is where Elliott Gaines was when he vanished," Jesse said as they pulled up to the spot.

Robin looked at the rocks with Xs on them and said, "Kind of spooky, huh?"

"Yeah," Jesse said. "It seems as if he just abandoned his Rover and walked into oblivion."

"Do you think that's what happened, Jesse?" Robin asked. "That he just lost it for some reason and then wandered off and fell into a canyon or something?"

"I wish I knew," Jesse admitted. "Say, Dr. Soto didn't mention anything about it last night, did she?"

"No," Robin said. "She just said that Elliott Gaines was a good friend of hers and that she felt terrible about what had happened. We talked mostly about plans for terraforming Mars. But all through the conversation, I got the feeling that she's grieving for Elliott. Like he was really, *really* important to her. I think she was in love with him."

"Yeah, I kind of got that feeling too," Jesse said. "I think I'll start my search today by circling the area in the Rover. Maybe I'll see a crevice or something that I missed yesterday."

"Fine," Robin said, climbing out of the Rover. "This looks like a perfect site for the terrarium. While you're driving, I'm going to sketch it out."

"Okay, I'll be back in a few minutes," Jesse said, waving good-bye to Robin.

He began driving around in a big circle. He noticed small mesas and some large boulders. But no crevices large enough to pose a safety hazard. Looking off into the distance at the mountains, Jesse thought he could easily be in New Mexico or Arizona. There were even some thin clouds covering the mountain peaks.

It would be nice if those were rain clouds, he thought. But then Mars would be a whole different place. He knew those thin clouds over the mountains were made of ice crystals and carbon dioxide ice.

It seemed clear that walking any reasonable distance in any direction would not have placed Elliott Gaines in any kind of danger. So maybe he *did* just keep walking and drop of exhaustion. If that happened, maybe the blowing red soil covered him like a blanket. Jesse looked around for any unusual mound that could be hiding a body, but he saw nothing.

Jesse returned to the original location then and found Robin propped on a rock, sketching.

"This is tough with these insulated gloves," Robin said, showing him her work. "But you get the general idea. The terrarium would be inflatable, of course. It would be as large as a sports arena and have a clear, plastic roof. Just think, Jesse, people could walk around in there and see fresh tomatoes on the vine and onions and radishes and leaf lettuce. We could have ponds of fish and eventually, of course, small animals. Poultry, rabbits, sheep. I think it would be so important to people to be able to walk around in such a place. It would make it seem like this was a real, living place instead of a bleak, dead planet." Robin paused and looked at Jesse. "You look as if you're a million miles away. Still thinking about Elliott Gaines?"

"Yeah," Jesse sighed. "It's just so frustrating that a guy vanishes into thin air. If he had died and we'd found his body, that would be one thing. But this—this disappearance. It's crazy."

"Yeah, I know," Robin said. "Last night some of the others were even joking about it. Alex Osgood suggested that there might be some weird lifeforms on Mars after all, and that they had abducted Elliott. Everyone laughed, except Dr. Soto. Guess I can't blame her—especially if she was in love with him."

"Do you mind if we just drive around a

BLOODRED SKY

while?" Jesse asked. "Maybe we'll see something that will give us some clues as to what happened."

"I don't mind at all," Robin replied, picking up her sketchpad. "I'm finished here, anyway."

They climbed into the Rover again and started off. Jesse drove slowly so they wouldn't miss anything—if there was anything to see.

A few minutes later, Robin cried out, "Jesse! Stop!"

"What is it?" Jesse asked, stopping the vehicle. They were about a mile from where Gaines had disappeared.

"That almost looks like tracks!" Robin said, pointing at the ground. "Like gigantic bird tracks."

"You're right. It does," Jesse said, squatting down to examine the prints. "But it must be something in the soil that makes it drift like that, don't you think?"

"Must be," Robin said. "I mean, there are no birds on Mars. We know that. There's *no* life on Mars."

Jesse had a funny feeling in the pit of his stomach. Nothing he had studied in his long preparation for the MEC II project had prepared him for this. Nothing he had learned answered the questions now swarming around in his mind. No class in Martian soil or geology explained the presence of these tracklike patterns.

Again, Jesse was baffled. It was totally impossible that there could be birds on Mars. It was as ridiculous as believing that dinosaurs were lurking in the redwood forests near his home. Preposterous.

But suddenly Jesse found himself arguing the impossible. "Look. The tracks seem purposeful . . . like they're headed somewhere."

"Maybe Gaines is playing some weird game," Robin suggested. "Maybe he put strange markings on the soles of his boots."

"But if he's still alive, where *is* he?" Jesse asked. "He's been missing for almost a week. His oxygen must have run out by now. And there's no water, no food. Nothing. These tracks look fresh, but there's no way he could have made them. Man, this is all so weird. *Too* weird."

"Yeah, it's giving me the creeps," Robin

said. "Can we go back now?"

"Sure," Jesse said. "I need to report these tracks to Dr. Chin anyway."

They drove back in silence, each pondering the mysterious tracks. When they reached the settlement, Jesse reported immediately to Dr. Chin.

"Last night, I read all the data gathered on the Rover," Jesse began. "Apparently, it had been in perfect working order. There's no sign that the Rover broke down or that Gaines's personal safety computer sent out an emergency signal."

Dr. Chin nodded. "Go on," he said.

"Today I inspected the site again where he vanished," Jesse continued. "He was not that far from the settlement. If his oxygen system had failed, he could have used the emergency supply in his pack. That would have given him at least 30 minutes to get back here, which would have been plenty of time. But, of course, he never showed up. Dr. Chin, are you sure Gaines went on that last expedition alone?"

"He had planned to," the commander replied. "He spoke to me about it the evening before. As you know, when colonists leave the settlement, they're required to fill out a detailed log of where they are going and when they expect to return. No one else filled out such a log, so I can only assume that Gaines was alone."

"The log says he was surveying large tracts of land for some future development," Jesse said.

"Yes, he and Dr. Soto believed there would eventually be a colony here with tens of thousands of people," Chin said. "Not everyone agrees, however. Like our military specialist, Colonel Coleman. He sees this colony as a defense outpost—nothing more than a tiny strategic site, should we ever need such a facility. You said you surveyed the site where Gaines disappeared again. Did you find anything unusual this time?"

"As a matter of fact, we did," Jesse replied. "I had Robin Palmer with me. She came along to look for a possible terrarium site. Anyway, about a mile from the site, Robin spotted what appeared to be . . . bird tracks."

Dr. Chin shook his head. "We've been through this before, Garcia," he said. "Obviously the wind and soil are playing tricks on us."

"I know, sir," Jesse replied. "That's what I told Robin. I just thought you should know what we found."

"Thank you for keeping me updated," Chin said. "By the way, keep these 'bird tracks' to yourself, will you? And ask Palmer to do the same. There's no reason to start any wild rumors. There's enough uneasiness about Gaines's disappearance as it is."

"Yes, sir," Jesse replied. "And I'll speak to Robin."

"Thank you," the commander said, escorting Jesse to the door.

During the next few days, Jesse made it a point to talk to all the colonists. His goal was to get a picture of the mindset of Elliott Gaines before he went on his expedition. Most of the colonists believed the young man was a bit strange. They thought his ideas were much too grandiose.

"He and Dr. Soto were living in a dream world," Colonel Artie Coleman said. "The United States government will never put out the money necessary to make this place a livable environment for thousands of people. We're here because it's a big prestige thing for our country. It's like years ago when the Russians launched Sputnik, and the Americans felt as if they had been beaten in the space race. Well, look at us now. We beat everyone else to Mars. We've done what we set out to prove—that we could do it. This place won't ever be home to a lot of people. It costs too darn much!"

"Colonel, what do *you* think happened to Elliott Gaines?" Jesse asked.

The colonel shrugged and said, "I think he was probably wandering around out there and lost track of time. He went out farther than he had planned and became confused. Maybe after that, he stumbled and hit his head on a rock or something. He's probably lying out there right now, covered by red Martian soil. And that's why we haven't found his body. Frankly, I don't think we ever will."

After talking with Colonel Coleman, Jesse went back to his apartment and settled down in his recliner. Robin had taken the Mars Rover out that morning for a second look at the terrarium site, but Jesse had seen all he wanted for right now. He wished he could neatly and definitely solve the mystery of Elliott Gaines's disappearance. But he was beginning to fear that he wouldn't be able to do that. He'd probably end up writing a report full of theories without a solid conclusion. Right now he was leaning toward the theory that Elliott Gaines had died of natural causes out there in the Utopian Plains, and, as Coleman had said, the wind had covered his body with red Martian soil.

4

Jesse heard an urgent knock on his door. When he answered it, Lara Soto was standing before him. Her eyes were wild with excitement.

"I need to talk to you!" she said.

"Okay, come on in," Jesse said.

"I'm sorry I was so rude to you the other night," she said. "It's just so awful having your sanity questioned by people you respect. And people you thought respected you!"

"I understand," Jesse said. "What did you want to talk about?"

"I think there is a plot afoot to destroy this colony," Lara said.

Jesse frowned. "A plot? What do you mean?"

"The disappearance of Elliott is causing the MEC II committee to have second thoughts," Dr. Soto explained. "Some of the members think the project should be postponed."

"Postponed?" Jesse repeated.

"Yes, the entire plan to make Mars a second Earth is in jeopardy, Jesse," the young woman said.

"And you think somebody in the colony is behind the plot?" Jesse asked.

"I . . . I didn't say that," Lara replied.

"Oh," Jesse said. "So what exactly—"

"We're not wanted here, Jesse," Lara said.

Suddenly Jesse realized what Dr. Soto was getting at. Somehow she thought alien forces were behind Gaines's disappearance. And that they had snatched—or killed—Gaines to scare Earthlings into abandoning the MEC project.

"Um, Lara . . ." Jesse began softly.

"There were important people supporting us," Lara raved on. "Members of Congress, senators, even the president was leaning our way. Important industrialists were starting to see commercial advantages to terraforming Mars. If we get picked off one by one, support from Earth will dry up. The news media will have a field day with it."

Jesse could understand what Lara was talking about. A handsome young scientist, Elliott Gaines, one of the super young people chosen for the program, was now a casualty of MEC. The media would give the story big play. There would be interviews with his weeping parents, his sister. They had all waved good-bye to Elliott five years earlier, and now the sinister red planet had claimed him. He was gone, and there was no explanation.

"It'll be like that time when the space shuttle exploded, killing the crew," Dr. Soto said. "Read the history of that! People were clamoring to end the space program. The same thing will happen now. They will say it is too dangerous to establish colonies on other planets. An incredibly important dream will vanish like a bubble, Jesse," Lara said. She lowered her voice then and added, "They don't want us here, Jesse, and this is how they plan to get rid of us!"

"The Martians?" Jesse asked.

"Don't use that patronizing tone of voice with me," Lara said bitterly. "You think you know it all, but you don't! We haven't *begun* to explore this planet. There are places we have never seen—

and never will. We can't say with absolute certainty that there are no life forms here. Life forms that might not wish to be disturbed!"

Jesse's imagination ran back to the movies he had seen as a child, the ridiculous old movies they showed on TV on Sunday afternoons. The disc-shaped flying saucers. The aliens with monkey paws and huge eyes or with multiple arms and heads. And then there were more recent films portraying an outer space filled with strange creatures warring against one another. But Jesse always saw those portrayals for what they were—fiction.

"Lara, there's nobody here with the intelligence to plot against us," Jesse said, trying to speak calmly. "Maybe someday we'll find simple plants or one-celled organisms under the ice caps. But there's no intelligent life on this planet now, and that's a certainty."

"*We're* here, aren't we?" the young woman pointed out.

"What do you mean?" Jesse asked.

"Well, we came from Earth," Dr. Soto

said. "Maybe there's someone *else* here from another planet. Some other race whose aim is to colonize Mars—just like ours. Maybe *they* want to drive us off."

"Look, Lara, our scientists have been studying this planet for decades," Jesse said. "Do you really think somebody else could be sending rockets here and we wouldn't know about it?"

"Why not?" Dr. Soto asked. "What if there's intelligent life in another galaxy? And what if they have developed some kind of space travel that's beyond our skill and knowledge? They wouldn't have to come in something as visible as a rocket, you know. What if there are other explorers here, and they don't want to share the exploration of Mars with us?"

Jesse thought that it was pretty obvious that Dr. Soto had been on Mars too long. Mars was a bizarre place. And the human personality could not function in bizarre situations very long. No human being before had ever been subjected to anything like MEC or MEC II. Explorers had sailed ships over oceans, but they remained in familiar environments. No part of the Earth was as different from another as Mars was from Earth. This was something totally new.

"Lara, I don't think anybody or anything harmed Elliott. I think the pressures of being here just got to him, and he started walking and became confused. It's like someone lost in the desert. They start hallucinating, and they walk in circles until they drop."

"You didn't even know him," Lara said bitterly. "I was with him every day, and I know how strong he was. He was growing more enthusiastic every day. The night before he vanished, we had a little party, just he and I, to celebrate our anniversary on this project. Five years since we set off from Earth. We were so happy and excited." Then suddenly, she said, "Come with me. I want to show you something."

Jesse followed Lara from his apartment down the hallway to another apartment. It occurred to Jesse that even the fact that they were living underground like gophers was hard on the mind. It was enough to unnerve anybody. Even gophers got to poke their heads out into the sunlight once in a while, to breathe fresh air. But the colonists had to cover themselves in all that protective gear to go out. And then all they saw was a red world without plants, without water, and without oxygen.

Lara led Jesse past her apartment. She stopped in front of another door farther down the hallway. "This is where he lived," she explained in a trembling voice.

Slowly, she pushed the door open. The walls of the apartment were decorated with beautiful paintings, romantic views of a Martian future. They featured soaring buildings, tall trees, and children playing with their pets beneath an artificial sky designed to filter out radiation.

"Elliott painted those," Lara said. "He was so talented. He wasn't just a scientist. He was gifted in so many things. He was an accomplished musician. He wrote poetry. He had such a great mind, such a vast imagination. Don't you see? It was so fitting that Elliott should come to Mars, to take part in this grand adventure. And so cruel, so awful that his promise should end here!"

"Okay, granted that Elliott Gaines was a bright, wonderful guy," Jesse admitted. "But the mind is a funny thing, Lara. Sometimes things just go awry. There's no other explanation."

Now, judging from Lara's intense emotion, Jesse knew she had been in love with Elliott Gaines. Jesse wished he could give her some hope that Gaines was still alive. That he might just come strolling back into the settlement one fine day. But that would be a lie. How could he still be alive after more than a week? This wasn't Earth. He could not have found a cool stream to drink from. He couldn't have found a berry bush to nourish himself. Or pulled a fish from the river. It wasn't like being lost in the Rocky Mountains. That was dangerous and even life-threatening—but not hopeless. Not like Mars. No one could survive on their own on Mars. Only men and women hunkered down in carefully protected underground shelters with specially designed life-support systems could survive here. And Gaines had disappeared out in the open on the Utopian Plains. And his support systems had to have run out long ago. Lara simply didn't want to face the truth that someone she loved had died.

"I'm really sorry, Lara," Jesse said quietly. "I can see that you cared a lot about Elliott. I'm really sorry this happened."

Dr. Soto shot a cold look at Jesse, as if she felt he really couldn't understand what she was going through.

"Well, I don't care how many people tell me that Elliott wandered off in some kind of a daze and then died of exposure," she insisted. "I won't believe it. Not Elliott. We are not wanted here. There were little clues even in the beginning. Mars Rovers not working right for no reason, as if they had been tampered with. Building materials taken. Just small things. We ignored them. We chalked it up to human error. But now I know it was more than that."

Lara shook her head. Then she began walking around the room, stopping at the various paintings. She touched one, a pastoral scene showing a winding river over a green meadow filled with flowers blooming. On the distant land, crops were growing.

"It could be just like Earth, you know," she sighed. "Little by little, we could build an atmosphere. Granted, it would take a very long time. But someday it could be like on the paintings. Mars could have blue skies and air to breathe, flowing rivers and wildlife. I'm telling you, Jesse. It can be done!"

Jesse thought about terraforming Mars. Some scientists proposed exploding powerful bombs underground to force the water from the ground, warming the planet. Other scientists discussed using mirrors in space to warm Mars. Once warmed, green plants could grow, and those plants would create oxygen for the atmosphere. But all that would take thousands of years. And it would cost a fortune. Jesse didn't know that it would *ever* happen. Mars might always be just a hostile outpost where humans could live only in very restricted quarters.

Then again, who knew? Only 150 years ago, the idea of reaching the moon was laughable. Who was to say for sure that humans wouldn't one day colonize Mars—and other planets, for that matter?

Suddenly the public address system broke into Jesse's thoughts. Dr. Chin's voice sounded urgent.

Will Robin Palmer please report to the communications room immediately? If Robin Palmer is anywhere in the settlement, she needs to report to me in the communications room.

Jesse turned numb as he remembered that Robin had taken the Rover out that morning. But that had been hours ago. It would be getting dark and cold on the Utopian Plains now. Surely she wasn't still out there.

5

Jesse hurried to the communications room. By the time he arrived, most of the other colonists were there. Several more came in after he did. A very upset Dr. Chin searched the group, obviously hoping to see Robin among them.

"We have searched the settlement for Robin Palmer," Dr. Chin said when they had all arrived. "She's not here. She took the Rover to the Utopian Plains today but had planned to return well before dark. As you can see, she is long overdue. We've had no communication from her since late this morning when she radioed in to tell us her location. I tried to reach her later, but she did not respond. I am very concerned. Very, *very* concerned."

"Just like Elliott Gaines," Alex Osgood said. "I'm telling you, this is getting spooky."

"Maybe she's just overdue," Jesse said, angry at Osgood for bringing up Gaines. It was just like Osgood to do such a thing. As if he delighted in being the bearer of bad news.

"Garcia," Dr. Chin said. "You and Osgood take a Rover out and see if you can find Robin. Report to me as soon as you get back."

"Yes, sir," both men replied.

"Let's go!" Jesse told Alex. "If she's still out there, there's a chance we can reach her before her support systems fail."

They suited up and then rushed to the above-ground exit. Outside, they climbed into a Rover and set out in the darkness. The battery-operated searchlights on the Rover threw eerie white light before them as they drove.

By the time they reached the last location Robin had radioed in from, the wind had picked up. Jesse could hear the sand particles bouncing off his suit and was glad for the protection. He knew that if those particles had actually been making contact, they would hurt!

"The wind is really kicking up!" Alex said. "Man, I used to think we had a lot of wind in North Dakota. But that's nothing compared to this!"

"Yeah, it's pretty constant here, isn't it?" Jesse replied.

Alex peered through the darkness at the bleak area surrounding them. "Do you see the Rover anywhere?"

"No," Jesse replied grimly. "No sign of it."

"Man, what are we doing in such a godforsaken place, anyway?" Alex asked dryly. "Are we crazy or what?"

"We spent four months in the orbiting space station, Alex," Jesse reminded him. "That should have told us if we could handle living in a Martian colony."

"I know, but that didn't prepare us for what this place is *really* like," Alex replied. "I had bad feelings about this mission all the way here. Then when we landed here, I started to get the creeps. The sense of isolation here is really extreme. You know the old saying 'nice place to visit, but I wouldn't like to live there'? Well, this isn't even a nice place to visit. Look—we can't even see where we're going with all the sand and dust blowing around."

"Take it easy, Alex. We're doing fine," Jesse said. "Just keep your eye out for the Rover."

"I've been in dust storms before, but this red stuff is murder," Alex said as the clouds of dust continued to envelop them. "I'm not sure we can make it much farther, Jesse."

"Alex, we've got to find her," Jesse said. "Maybe the Rover stalled, and her communication system broke down. She could be sitting out here just waiting for help to arrive."

Suddenly Alex yelled, "Look! There it is!"

As they approached the Rover, Jesse could see that it was empty. "Keep your eye out for Robin!" he told Alex as he got out to inspect the vehicle.

The tires of the Rover were half-buried in blowing dirt. It had apparently been there for hours. Jesse jumped into the driver's seat and tried to start it. It ran perfectly!

Despair clawed at Jesse. Why would Robin abandon the Rover? he wondered. Where was she? She couldn't have just wandered off as everyone thought Gaines had done. It was too coincidental to have two people do that within a few days of each other. Besides, she had only been here a few days. Not long enough to be depressed or driven to despair by the strange environment she had found herself in.

"She *must* be nearby," he said, feeling his stomach grow sick with fear. "Maybe she's injured or something. Look around! We can't leave her!"

They spent the next few minutes combing the area, being careful not to wander too far from the lights of their Rover.

Finally Alex said, "Jesse, come on, we'd better go. The storm is getting worse. We've got to get back to the settlement, or we'll be lost too!"

"We can't leave her out here, Alex!" Jesse cried. "She's our friend!"

"She's not here," Alex answered. "At least not in this immediate vicinity. And if we wander off too far, we'll be lost too. Come on. Get back in the Rover. We've got to get moving. Should one of us drive her vehicle back?"

Jesse sighed and shook his head. How could it be? he wondered. How could Robin have disappeared too? And did it have anything to do with Gaines? Dr. Soto's grim warning came back to haunt him. *We're not wanted here.*

"No, leave the Rover here in case she comes back," Jesse replied. "She'll need it."

Jesse let Alex drive back to the settlement. He knew he was too upset to drive. And he wanted to keep an eye out for Robin in case she was wandering around.

"This is really a nasty place," Alex said, struggling against the rough terrain and the clouds of dust. "Those guys who decided to colonize Mars must be short some brain cells. It's a big, monstrous, ugly desert."

"Alex, I feel so bad about going back to the settlement without Robin," Jesse groaned. "It's like we abandoned her out there."

"We had no choice, Jesse," Alex said flatly. "Besides, she's not out there anyway. You know it. I know it."

"Then where is she?" Jesse cried.

"The same place Gaines is, would be my guess," Alex said. "Where that is, though, I don't know."

When Jesse and Alex returned to the settlement, they joined the waiting colonists in the communications room.

"What did you find?" Dr. Chin asked guardedly.

"Just the empty Rover," Jesse said. "We combed the area—as much as we could, what with the wind and blowing sand. But we saw no sign of her. We left the Rover there, in case she comes back."

"You're saying that her vehicle works fine then?" Dr. Chin asked. "So did Gaines's."

Lara stepped forward. "Did you see any tracks?" she demanded.

"Dr. Soto, not now!" the commander groaned.

"*Especially* now!" Lara cried. She turned back to Jesse and Alex. "Well? Did you see any?"

"It was dark. And the dust storm was so bad we couldn't see anything," Jesse said.

"What are you talking about? Tracks?" Alex demanded.

"It's all absurd," Dr. Chin said hastily.

"It is *not* absurd," Lara cried. "With all due respect, sir, when are you going to face the facts? How many of us have to disappear before you realize the danger we're in?"

"Dr. Soto, I'm ordering you to be silent," Dr. Chin said. "I'll have no more of your ridiculous theory. If you persist, I'll place a letter of censure in your file, and MEC officials will be informed of it. Believe me, your career in the space program will then be over."

Lara laughed bitterly and said, "I think we should all be beyond caring about our careers in space! Our lives are on the line here."

"What *are* you talking about?" Alex demanded again.

Lara turned to Alex. "I found some strange tracks in the soil where Elliott disappeared. I measured them. I photographed them. They were like bird tracks. And they led to and away from the Rover."

"Bird tracks!" Alex replied in surprise. "But there hasn't been life on Mars for millions of years—if there *ever* was. How could we be dealing with giant birds?"

"Do you see?" Dr. Chin cried. "It's all fanciful nonsense." He turned then to Rashid Cheddi, the team's medical doctor. "Dr. Cheddi, please accompany Dr. Soto to her apartment and administer a sedative to her."

"I don't need a sedative!" Lara snapped. "Something took Elliott away, and now it has taken Robin away. Those are the facts. And they're *not* fanciful nonsense!"

Bianca Forest stepped forward then. "Dr. Chin, maybe Lara is right. Something terrible has happened. Now, we can ridicule her theories all we want, but nobody has a better explanation for the loss of two of our colleagues!"

"Yeah," Steve Saunders said. "We've got the right to know what we're up against here. We shouldn't dismiss anyone's theories until we're sure."

"People, this is no time for mass hysteria," Dr. Chin said. "Both Gaines and Palmer were apparently suffering from disorientation. Maybe something in the oxygen masks is flawed. You can be assured that we will be checking and double-checking everything. And from now on, *no one* is to venture out onto the surface alone. When you leave the settlement in a Rover, you will travel in pairs. No exceptions! This is a great tragedy. But if we allow insane fears to unhinge our minds, then the entire project could be scrapped. That would be an even greater tragedy because we've all worked so hard and sacrificed so much."

Bianca ignored the commander and turned to Dr. Soto. "Give us more details about your theory, Lara."

"I believe there are creatures on this planet who do not want us here," Lara said. "I don't know what they are or where they are from, but they've taken Elliott and now Robin. And they might be planning to get us all!"

"And you think they might be birds—giant birds?" Steve Saunders asked.

"Do you see how we are descending into madness?" Dr. Chin cried. "The best thing we can do is return to our apartments and get a good night's sleep. Then we can examine the situation with clear heads tomorrow."

But the discussion persisted.

Another of the colonists said, "Maybe there are natural hazards on Mars that we don't know about yet. Like sinkholes, where the land just completely gives way. Elliott and Robin could have been walking around, and the planet just swallowed them up. That would explain their vanishing without a trace."

"Now *that's* a theory that makes some sense," Dr. Chin said eagerly. "We'll look into it as soon as we can. In the meantime, when we travel on the surface, we'll be joined by a tether so that if one should fall into a crevice, the companion can pull him out."

"So," Saunders said, still clinging to the bird theory, "you think giant birds—or something similar—carried off two of our crew. Well, if that's true, where would such things come from?"

Dr. Chin looked stricken that the giant bird theory was once more on the table.

"I don't know," Lara said. "Maybe they were brought by explorers from another galaxy. Maybe they *are* the explorers themselves. But it's not too outrageous to think that someone else might be exploring the possibilities of colonizing Mars at the same time we are. We don't exactly have exclusive rights to space exploration, you know."

Steve Saunders finally shook his head. "I am getting a very weird picture here. We've got some aliens who have landed on Mars, and they're sending around giant birds to snatch up our people. Or they, themselves, *are* giant birds. I don't know what the rest of you think, but I'm getting the feeling some of us are going off the deep end here."

"Exactly," Dr. Chin exclaimed, obviously delighted by the support. "This is all madness. There are no aliens. There are no giant birds. There are only fevered imaginations. Dr. Soto, it pains me to say this, but you must leave the colony. In two months the supply ship will be coming back. When it leaves for Earth, you must be on it. You've done excellent work here, and it hurts me to dismiss you from MEC II. But it is for the good of the colony and for your own good as well."

Lara glared at the commander. "I will *not* leave here until I know what happened to Elliott. He was my friend. He was my life! And I will not abandon whatever is left of him to this horrid place! I'd spend the rest of my life haunted by the fear that he is marooned here without hope, wondering why I left."

Tears began streaming down her face then. Bianca put her arm around Dr. Soto's shoulders to comfort her.

"I will not leave without Elliott," Lara sobbed. "Dead or alive—I will not leave him here!"

6

The next afternoon Jesse was in the recreation room of the settlement playing computer games. He had wanted to go to the surface again to look for Robin. But Dr. Chin refused his request. Chin had ordered everyone to take time out daily for recreation. He thought regular relaxation might prevent them all from burning out.

"Especially you, Garcia," Chin had said. "You've been working extra hard because you're trying to get to the bottom of this. I'm sending Saunders and Cheddi to look for Robin. You take some time out to relax."

Jesse looked up as Bianca Forest entered the rec room.

"Hi, Bianca," Jesse said.

"Hi, Jesse," Bianca replied, turning on another computer and sitting down to play a game. "How are you doing?"

"Okay, I guess, all things considered," he replied. "I'm having a hard time concentrating on this game, though. It's hard to relax when so many scary things are going on."

"I know," Bianca sighed. She stared at her screen for a few minutes and then asked, "Jesse, do you think there's really intelligent life anywhere else in the universe—besides on Earth, I mean?"

Jesse shrugged. "I don't know. I've always wondered about it and sort of figured there wasn't, but I'm not sure why. You know, there are scientists—brilliant scientists—aiming radio telescopes into space every hour of the day looking for messages from other galaxies. It's been going on for decades, so *they* must think it's possible that somebody else is out there."

"You remember studying about past space missions?" Bianca asked. "Remember, that back in the 1970s, two spacecrafts were launched from Earth—*Pioneer 10* and *Pioneer 11*? They were supposed to fly past Jupiter and Saturn and then go right on into the solar system toward the stars. Scientists were hoping that the crafts would reach other galaxies.

In case they did, they enclosed a plaque in each. The plaques were about six inches wide by nine inches long and were made of gold. They had a map of our solar system drawn on them. Then they had a picture of a spacecraft and a man and a woman. The man in the picture had his hand raised, as if he were greeting someone. The scientists figured that if anybody out there in space found one of the plaques, they would be able to tell where the probe had come from. And they'd be able to see what humans looked like and to tell that they were amicable beings."

Bianca returned to her game for a few minutes. Then she said, "I don't believe there are big, mean birds out there though, do you?"

"No. I don't buy it either," Jesse said.

"But what if it's true?" Bianca asked. "I was camping in the mountains once with my parents, and I saw this great big eagle come swooping down and snatch up a hare in its claws. I was so terrified. Of course I was just a little kid, but I cried and cried. Now I'm thinking, if there would be something like that eagle around here, only bigger, and it swooped down and grabbed up people, that would be terrible. Too terrible to even think about. Poor Elliott and Robin!"

Jesse smiled then and said, "First of all, if the tracks are right, the birds didn't swoop down and snatch anyone up. The tracks seemed to indicate that the birds carried something away."

"Do you think that's what happened to Elliott and Robin?" Bianca wanted to know.

"No, but I don't know what *did* happen," Jesse replied. "I think Dr. Chin is right when he says that people can go nuts in a place like this and just wander off into the wilderness. But it's a little too much of a coincidence to think that two people did that in the last few days."

"Yeah, I didn't know Elliott, but I can't imagine such a thing happening to Robin," Bianca agreed. "She was too levelheaded. I've known Robin all through the space program. We trained together. Nothing fazes her. She's always been steady as a rock. When we were all struggling with weightlessness and nausea and some of us were freaking out, she was cool. She took it all in stride."

Jesse nodded. "I know. She'd be one of the last people I'd suspect of being mentally unstable."

Just then Steve Saunders entered the room.

"Did you find anything out there?" Jesse asked immediately. "Any sign of Robin?"

Saunders shook his head and turned on another computer. "Nothing," he replied. "It's as if she just vanished into the atmosphere. We had to come back because it's getting dark."

"Hey, Jesse, do you want to go to the observatory and watch Phobos set?" Bianca asked. "It's supposed to be really pretty."

"Sure," Jesse said. "I'm tired of these games anyway. See you later, Steve."

"So long," Saunders answered, not looking up from his game.

Jesse had always been fascinated by the journey of Phobos. It rose in the west and set in the east three times a day. Because it was so close to Mars, it whipped around the planet rapidly, unlike

Earth's moon, which rose and set just once a day. But, like the Earth's moon, Phobos appeared like a disk. The other Martian moon, Deimos, looked like a bright star in the sky.

In the observatory, Jesse and Bianca sat in recliners and stared up at the pink sky.

"There it is," Bianca said. "Pretty dramatic, huh?"

"Yeah, no atmosphere to blur it," Jesse said. He glanced over at Bianca then. Her eyes shone as she gazed up at the sky. During the flight to Mars, Jesse had developed special feelings for Bianca. He had kept them hidden because he didn't want his feelings to interfere with the job they had of getting the ship to Mars. Now he wondered if Bianca felt the same way about him. He hoped so.

They were silent until the moon was gone. Then a great white afterglow spread over the sky, making the horizon appear sharply black.

Bianca caught her breath at the sight. "Isn't that beautiful?" she asked.

"Yeah. Moonset on Mars," Jesse said. "It's something we can all tell our children about. Unless they're already here, living in one of those skyscrapers being planned."

"I could never live here permanently," Bianca said.

"I couldn't either," Jesse agreed.

"When the next supply ship comes, I might just be on it when it leaves," Bianca admitted. "I had planned on staying a year. But what happened to Robin has changed all that. I have a family in Texas. Mom and Dad and my sisters. I mean, they want to see me again, and I want to see them. This place is getting too dangerous for my tastes."

"I wonder if what that one guy said about holes in the ground could be true," Jesse mused. "Like quicksand that just opens up and down you go."

"But the soil is so hard and rocky," Bianca said. "I can't imagine there being any sinkholes."

Jesse continued looking up at the sky. Suddenly he saw something move.

"What's that?" he asked

"What's what?" Bianca asked. "Did you see something?"

Jesse stood up and peered outside. "Something just drifted through the sky and bounced on the observatory roof, real softly," he said.

"What did it look like?" Bianca asked.

Jesse didn't want to say what it looked like. "Bianca, I'm going out there. I'm going to try to find what I saw."

"But what did it look like?" Bianca asked again.

But Jesse was already headed to get his suit and oxygen mask on. He left the comfortable, controlled environment of the settlement and went into the bitter cold Martian night. Since there was no atmosphere to hold the daytime heat, the coldness settled in much more rapidly. It could quickly go from scorching hot to dangerously cold in a matter of minutes. Luckily, Jesse's suit protected him from such temperature extremes.

Jesse walked carefully over the rock-strewn land, trying to locate the thing he had seen. He threw his flashlight beam around the soil. Finally he spotted it. A pure white feather about six feet long lay against a rock a few feet away.

With gloved hands that were trembling, Jesse picked up the feather. It was exactly like a bird's feather. And, like a bird's feather, it weighed almost nothing, despite its size. Jesse returned to the settlement with the feather. Bianca was waiting for him.

"What did you find?" she asked anxiously as he removed his helmet.

"This," Jesse said. He showed her the feather.

Bianca's eyes widened, and she paled. "But . . . what *is* that?"

"If I'm not mistaken, it's a feather," Jesse replied. "A bird feather."

"But it's not for real, is it?" Bianca asked, still stunned. "I mean, it couldn't be. It must be a hoax."

"I don't think so," Jesse said.

"Jesse, are you saying—" Bianca gasped.

"I don't know what I'm saying," Jesse said. "But we'd better go see Dr. Chin."

Together they hurried to Dr. Chin's quarters.

"I hope you got in some recreation time today," Dr. Chin said pleasantly when he opened his door.

BLOODRED SKY

"Dr. Chin, we need to talk," Jesse said.

Dr. Chin's smile faded. "Come in," he said.

Jesse showed Dr. Chin the feather he was carrying. Dr. Chin stared at the object and said, "What is this? Where did you get that?"

"On the surface," Jesse said. "I saw it come down from the observatory. Bianca was with me. I went out and got it."

"It can't be what it seems to be. It must be some joke," Dr. Chin said.

"Dr. Chin, let's have Newhall examine it in the lab," Jesse suggested. "She'll be able to tell if it's from a living organism or if it's a hoax."

"You're right," Dr. Chin said. He buzzed Rebecca Newhall, and in moments the young biologist/chemist appeared. Jesse told her what had happened. Newhall looked at the feather in surprise and said, "Do you think this is related to what Dr. Soto has been talking about—the bird tracks?"

"No," the commander said quickly. "I'm sure someone in the colony made this object and planted it as a hoax."

Newhall nodded. "Well, there's only one way to find out. I'll go to work on it right away, and then we'll know exactly what we're dealing with."

Jesse returned alone to his apartment, shaken by the discovery. He had been so excited about his year in the Martian colony, the important work he would be doing. But now fear was overcoming his enthusiasm. If there truly was something out there trying to destroy the colony, then how could he concentrate on his normal tasks? If it became a struggle for survival, what was the sense of going on with MEC II?

Jesse threw himself down on the bed and waited.

****

Much later that evening, Dr. Chin came to Jesse's apartment. Dr. Chin was in a high state of anxiety. He was more upset than Jesse had ever seen him.

"The preliminary tests indicate that the . . . feather . . . is from a living organism," the older man said. "Newhall will conduct more tests, of course. But it's unlike anything she has seen before. The DNA is different, but the appearance and structure are the same."

Jesse shook his head and ran his hand through his hair. "How can it be?" he wondered aloud.

"Let me remind you, Garcia, these findings are not definite," Dr. Chin said. "We must continue to investigate, to see if there is some logical explanation. In the meantime, both you and Forest are to keep this information to yourselves. To do otherwise could cause hysteria. Until now, most of the crew has dismissed Soto's claims of finding bird tracks as nonsense. Let's leave it that way."

"But, Dr. Chin, don't you think the others deserve the truth?" Jesse asked.

"We don't *know* the truth yet, Garcia," Chin replied. "This Martian colony has been the dream of my life. I couldn't bear to see it come to an end because of some unfounded fears. Do I make myself clear?"

"Of course, sir," Jesse said. "I'll tell no one."

But Jesse wasn't sure he'd be able to keep his promise. If one more colonist disappeared or anything else weird happened, he would feel it was his duty to inform the others. Dr. Chin was a good man. But more was at stake now than his dream. Maybe all of their lives were at stake.

7

In the morning Dr. Chin met with a small group of his most trusted colonists. He had to include Jesse and Bianca because they had discovered the feather. Also at the meeting were Rebecca Newhall and Colonel Coleman.

"If there are indeed creatures from who-knows-where around here, none of us can leave the settlement unarmed," Colonel Coleman said briskly. His face was flushed with energy. "Unfortunately, defense rather than scientific inquiry now seems to be the order of the day. From now on, every one of us must carry weapons."

"But what do we know about weapons?" Bianca asked.

"Garcia here has military training, and I do, of course," the colonel said. "We will train everyone."

Jesse had gone through the military cadet program in high school and college. But the thought of having to prepare for violence stunned him. There had been peace on Earth for decades. And he had never expected to have to use his training against beings from outer space.

"In the meantime, no one leaves the settlement unless either Garcia or I accompany them," Coleman added.

"What will we tell the others?" Bianca asked. "Won't they wonder why suddenly they're being expected to know how to handle a weapon?"

The colonel shrugged. "We'll tell them it's simply a precaution until we get to the bottom of what happened to Palmer and Gaines. After all, it's for their own good."

During the next few days, everyone received training in the use of firearms. First, Colonel Coleman updated Jesse, and then the two of them began training the others. Until everyone was properly trained, the only two allowed to carry guns were the colonel and Jesse.

"I'm not surprised by this development," Coleman told Jesse during one of the training sessions.

"You mean you thought there'd be hostile forces on Mars?" Jesse asked in amazement. "Nobody talked about such a thing at MEC headquarters in Florida. We've known for ages that Mars is a cold, lifeless planet. Why should we have expected enemies?"

To himself, Jesse thought that had he known anything like this would happen, he never would have signed on for the mission. This was to be the peaceful colonization of a dead planet, with the hopes of someday making it a new Earth.

"I'm not convinced that the enemy is not from within," Coleman said grimly.

"One of the other colonists, you mean?" Jesse asked.

"It's possible," the colonel replied. "The human mind is a dark place indeed. There may be a spy in our midst with a mission to destroy MEC II."

"But the feather. Where would something like that come from?" Jesse asked.

"I'm not sure such a thing could not be cleverly made, integrating animal matter and synthetic substances," Coleman said. "Surely it would be a dramatic way to undermine the morale of the colony.

Newhall has more tests to conduct. She may find it's a hoax. Jesse, did you ever take anthropology in college?"

"Yes, I did," Jesse said.

"Then you may have learned about the Piltdown Man," the colonel continued. "It was all a hoax. Anthropologists were trying to find the missing link between apes and humans. Well, some of them got tired of waiting, so they built this creature from a man's skull and the skull of an orangutan. They fooled everyone for quite a while. But eventually the creature was exposed as a fraud. Well, this might be the same kind of thing. Someone could have planted that feather. If so, it's probably the same person who caused the disappearance of Gaines and Palmer. We'll see. In the meantime, we have to be prepared for anything. If you take one of the colonists out in a Rover and you are accosted by anyone or anything, you know what to do!"

Jesse returned to his apartment in the evening. A little while later, Bianca stopped by. They drank coffee and talked.

"You know, I think I might leave too

when the supply ship comes," Jesse confided.

"Yeah," Bianca said. "Finding that giant feather decided it for me. I mean, I was really excited about developing the terrarium with Robin, but with her gone, I'm thinking maybe the whole MEC II is a big mistake. Maybe we're not supposed to be here. Maybe we should be solving the problems on Earth first instead of trying to colonize other planets. Maybe we should be spending the money on curing disease and poverty instead of using it for space travel."

Jesse was surprised to see how completely Bianca was turning against the project. But he realized that he, too, was leaning that way. They could fight the environment, the cold, and the isolation of this strange planet. But they couldn't fight an alien force that was capable of snatching two people without a trace. Just the thought of such a threat was probably enough to drive some of them over the deep end.

****

The next morning, Jesse accompanied Lara Soto on her exploration of the outer edges of the Utopian Plains. Before leaving, he tucked his weapon out of sight.

"Jesse," Lara said as she pulled away in the Rover. "I talked to Bianca Forest this morning at breakfast. I got the feeling that she had something on her mind. Something she didn't want to talk about. She's always so bright and cheerful, but this morning she was almost gloomy."

"She's just stressed out about Robin. They were good friends," Jesse said.

"I know that, but she looks suspicious. Like she's hiding something," Dr. Soto insisted.

"I guess we're all feeling pretty weird," Jesse said, avoiding her eyes. "None of us is probably acting like ourselves."

The young woman shook her head. "No, it's more than that," she said. "Has something happened that I should know about? I have the sense that something is being kept from me. I also noticed that Rebecca is very busy in her lab. I asked her what she was doing, and she put me off too."

"She's . . . um . . . testing soil samples, I think," Jesse said.

"She's been doing that ever since she got here," Lara said, narrowing her eyes in suspicion. "That's nothing new. No, something else is going on. Dr. Chin has an inner circle of people now. And he's funneling information to them and leaving the rest of us in the dark."

"Lara, nothing like that is going on," Jesse insisted. He hated to be part of a cover-up, but Dr. Chin had sworn him and the others to secrecy for now.

"I know I said I wouldn't leave here without Elliott's remains, but I've changed my mind," Lara said. "When trust is dead among the members of a group, there's no point in sticking around. I'm going back to Earth, just as Dr. Chin wants. I think everyone else should go too. Chin is the commander on a doomed ship, and he refuses to see it."

She maneuvered the Mars Rover around some rocks and then parked near a vast depression in the land. They both got out and, at least for the moment, Dr. Soto became a scientist again.

"A meteor struck here," Lara said, pointing to the area around them. "It was about the size of a football field. Not enormous for meteors but still very destructive. Elliott was concerned about protecting Worldcity from meteors. He felt that by studying the impact of past meteor strikes, we could develop a way to deflect incoming ones. He knew that if an incoming meteor were to strike the roof of the city, it would be disastrous, Radiation would pour in, causing the deaths of everyone here." She shook her head and sighed. "Oh, how he worried about that. And now it seems likely that none of it will happen."

Jesse knew what Dr. Soto was feeling. If the colony were simply abandoned, everything they—and many others—had worked for would be lost. A feeling of keen disappointment seeped through him. Like everyone else involved, he wanted this to be a great experience. He wanted his year here and a lifetime of memories he could take with him when it was over.

"I'm so sorry about what's happening here," Jesse said.

"Me too," Dr. Soto replied. "It would have been so glorious!"

Jesse glanced up then and gasped. His heart almost stopped. Something was far off, circling in the sky.

"Lara! Look," Jesse cried.

"What is that?" Lara exclaimed. "Jesse—it's a bird. A huge bird!"

Jesse struggled against the panic building up in his chest. "Quick! Under the Rover!" he shouted. He grasped Lara's hand, and they bounded, stumbling over the Martian soil. They made it to the Rover and crawled underneath the tractorlike vehicle.

"It's going to get us," Lara said hoarsely. "It will crawl under here after us!"

"No, no," Jesse said. "I have a weapon. I'll use it if I have to." He crouched under the Rover with Lara, watching the lowering circles of the great bird. He could not make out any features yet, only its silvery white color.

"If it gets any closer, I'm going to fire a warning shot," Jesse said. "Maybe I can scare it off. It probably thinks we're unarmed like the others."

Jesse shocked himself by talking about the bird as if he already knew it had high intelligence. He wasn't seeing the creature as a large bird. It was more than that. It was a creature who wanted the humans off Mars.

"Jesse," Lara moaned. "Oh, Jesse!"

As the birdlike creature drew nearer, Jesse estimated its length was about 20 feet and its wingspan 40 to 50 feet. Jesse's gloved hand closed on the automatic weapon he carried.

Soon Jesse could hear the great wings beating. It was now just above them. Jesse fired his gun across the empty Martian plain. The explosion startled the creature. It wavered in the sky, as if in indecision. But then it recovered itself and came even closer.

"Jesse, it's coming!" Lara screamed.

Perspiration streamed down Jesse's face as he prepared to fire again.

8

"Shoot! Jesse, shoot!" Lara cried. Suddenly, the huge creature rose in the sky again.

"I think it's going away," Jesse said. "Yes, look. It's veering around and leaving." Quickly, he crawled out from underneath the Rover and grabbed a pair of binoculars on the seat. He peered at the bird before it completely turned away from them.

"Jesse! The creature's face. It was almost . . . humanlike," Dr. Soto began as she scrambled out from under the vehicle.

"I know," Jesse said, lowering the binoculars. "And under its wings it had armlike limbs."

"But how can that be?" Lara asked.

"It wasn't wearing a mask, either," Jesse said. "It must be able to tolerate the Martian atmosphere."

The bird was now some distance away, but it was circling lower, as if preparing to land. It glided down, its wings beating faster as it approached the surface of the planet. Jesse and Lara lost sight of it for a few minutes, and then suddenly it rose again.

"Jesse, it's coming back!" Lara cried.

Jesse held his weapon in readiness, but he did not want to use it. The creature did not seem like a bird of prey. It seemed to act on intelligence rather than instinct. Shooting it would be like shooting intelligent life, a *person* of some kind.

"It's getting closer, Jesse," Lara said, panic rising in her voice. She squatted down, ready to dive under the Rover again if necessary.

Jesse fired his weapon into the air and the creature retreated again. This time it spiraled higher and higher. Finally, it disappeared from view.

"Let's get out of here," Jesse said, scrambling to get into the Rover. Lara climbed behind the wheel and drove away.

As the Rover bounced along the rocky terrain, Jesse and Lara said nothing to each other. But they kept glancing up into the sky to reassure themselves that the creature had not returned.

When they were almost at the settlement, Lara broke the silence. "You see?" she said accusingly. "The bird tracks *were* real. They got Elliott and Robin. They want us off this planet."

"But what are they? Where do they come from?" Jesse wondered aloud.

"Who knows?" Lara said. "They're probably space travelers like us. We watched those space movies growing up, those movies filled with strange creatures who supposedly lived in distant galaxies. We should have guessed it would happen eventually—that there would be contact somewhere, somehow. The universe doesn't belong just to us. These creatures may be far ahead of us in technology. They probably see us as we see squirrels and monkeys. As inferior beings. They're probably . . . studying Elliott and Robin." Her voice broke then, and she stopped.

"Don't torture yourself with things you don't even know are true," Jesse said.

Dr. Soto was quiet for the rest of the trip. When they reached the settlement, they hurried to find Dr. Chin.

"We saw one of the creatures," Jesse said. "It was about 20 feet long, with a wingspan of 40 or 50 feet. It circled our Rover and then flew away."

"They really *are* gigantic birds, then?" Dr. Chin asked, stunned.

"Yes, just as I said," Dr. Soto replied.

"Dr. Soto, please forgive me for doubting you," the commander implored.

"There's more, Dr. Chin," Jesse said. "The creature had a . . . humanlike face. And arms. And it was definitely intelligent."

"What?!" Dr. Chin demanded. "First you tell me there are giant birds flying around Mars. And now you tell me they look like *us*? How can that be? How can one species look like two?"

"Obviously, they evolved differently, Dr. Chin," Dr. Soto said. "Somehow two species were crossed. Similar mix-ups, although not nearly as drastic, have occurred on Earth. So why not somewhere else?"

Dr. Chin sat down heavily. "This is a disaster for MEC II. A complete disaster." He buried his face in his hands for a minute. Then he pulled himself together. "No one can be allowed to leave the settlement. *No one*!" he said. "I'm calling a meeting of all staff immediately!"

A few minutes later, the rest of the crew had gathered together. Jesse and Lara briefly explained what they had seen.

Bianca asked, "Was the creature hostile?"

"We assume so," Lara replied. "It circled our location, as if waiting for the chance to snatch us up."

"I fired my weapon into the air and scared it off," Jesse said.

"Any sign of others?" Colonel Coleman asked.

"No, we saw only the one creature," Jesse replied.

"Well, where there's one, there's probably more, many more," the colonel said. "And if they have weapons, we're not armed well enough to withstand a full-scale attack. The best thing to do for now is to simply stay below."

"I agree," Dr. Chin said. "*Everyone* is restricted to the underground buildings. We must remain out of sight and reinforce the exits. If they break through and swarm over us, we have to defend ourselves as best we can. If we can hold out for two months, the supply ship will be here. At that time, we will all depart for Earth."

"Will there be enough supplies aboard the ship to sustain us all for the trip back to Earth?" Jimmy Manning asked.

"Yes," Dr. Chin said. "We'll take supplies from the settlement too. It won't be a pleasant journey. We'll be crowded. And we'll have to live with the fact that our dream has failed. But we'll be alive. And that's all that matters."

"It's almost seven weeks until the supply ship comes," Alex said. "What if they swarm down on us before then?"

"I told you, we'll defend ourselves as best we can," Dr. Chin said wearily.

"We can beat off some of them," Colonel Coleman said. "But if there are hundreds, we're lost. They'll overwhelm us. We did not come here prepared for war."

The anxious questioning continued, but Jesse had had enough. He walked back to his apartment, tired and frightened. He sat down in his reclining chair in the bedroom and dozed off. He dreamed of Redwood City. It was a lovely spring day, and he was driving to San Francisco. Bianca Forest was with him, and they were crossing the Golden Gate Bridge. After they got off the bridge, they stopped and walked hand-in-hand along a beach. Seagulls began to appear a few at a time. They were not ordinary seagulls though. They were enormous birds, and there were so many that they blotted out the sun.

"Jesse, they're after us!" Bianca screamed.

The seagulls were so close overhead that their white wings brushed Jesse's and Bianca's hair. But it was a gentle action. And you could see by the kindly looks in the eyes of the birds that they were only playing.

Jesse awoke with a start. "What a dream!" he mumbled.

He settled back into the recliner again but couldn't sleep. He decided to go to the observatory and watch the sky for a while. He didn't care that he was supposed to be restricted to the underground buildings. He had to find a place to think.

From under the great, domed structure, Jesse watched as the ever-changing Martian sky went from pink to bloodred then back to pink again. He was enjoying the show, but suddenly the sky was blocked out. Jesse heard a light thud and looked up to see one of the creatures landing on the dome. Its huge wingspan blocked out what light remained in the sky. Then the sky reappeared as the creature folded its wings against itself.

Jesse slowly got to his feet. He swallowed hard against the rising tide of panic he felt within him. He forced himself to remain calm. He grasped the microphone in the observatory and spoke into it, hoping the creature outside would somehow understand.

"Who are you, and what do you want?" Jesse asked.

There appeared to be some kind of device on the creature's chest, the size of a small calculator. The device lit up now, as if it were receiving a signal. Soon, a mechanical voice, speaking in English, said, "What do *you* want?"

Jesse stared at the creature, trying to

figure out what was happening. Maybe the device was a translator. Maybe it took whatever language it heard and translated the words into its own language. Then it replied in the other person's language.

"We are explorers from the planet Earth. We have come to Mars peacefully. We want to study Mars," Jesse said.

The device glowed again. "We search the realms of the stars to learn," the voice said.

"Where are Elliott Gaines and Robin Palmer? They are our friends. Do you know where they are?" Jesse asked.

There was a long period of time before a reply came. "Come with me," said the voice.

Jesse shook his head. "What did you do with my friends?" he asked.

The creature stared at Jesse with curiosity and repeated its command. "Come with me."

But Jesse shook his head. "Tell me where my friends are," he said.

This time the creature did not reply. But from underneath its wing, it raised its handlike limb. It looked as if it was about to deliver a blow to the transparent roof.

Jesse shrank back and prepared to head for the exit to the underground buildings. If the creature penetrated the roof, Jesse would have to abandon the observatory immediately to escape the sun's radiation.

But the creature did not strike the roof. It held its right hand aloft and moved it back and forth in a strange manner, almost like someone in a parade waving to fans. It was such a strange gesture from this alien creature that Jesse did not know what to make of it. Finally the creature lowered its arm, spread its gigantic wings again, and vanished into the night.

Jesse rushed closer to the observation window and watched the creature fly away. Its giant, broad wings beat loudly as it rose higher and higher into the sky. Suddenly Jesse realized he had been holding his breath. He emptied his lungs with a rush. He wondered what had just happened. He was frightened and awed and totally confused.

Just at that moment, Alex Osgood appeared. "I thought I saw you sneak up here. What do you think you're doing?" he asked Jesse.

BLOODRED SKY

Jesse was still so stunned, he couldn't reply. "Hey, what's the matter, Garcia?" Alex asked. "You look like you've seen another one of those big birds you were talking about."

Jesse nodded mutely.

"You really *did* see another one?" Alex asked in amazement. "Oh, man, this is crazy. What happened?"

"One of the bird creatures came to the roof of the observatory," Jesse said, his voice still shaky.

"Was it the same one you saw earlier?" Alex wanted to know.

"I don't know," Jesse said. "Maybe."

"I'll be right back," Alex said, heading for the exit. "Don't go *anywhere!*"

A few minutes later, Alex was back with Colonel Coleman. The colonel's face was red with fury. His words poured out of him. "You say the observatory was attacked, Garcia? What did you do? Are you hurt? Why didn't you call me to help?"

"It didn't attack the observatory," Jesse said. "It just landed on the roof and looked in at me. It was so strange. It communicated with me in English."

"You mean you talked to it?" Coleman demanded.

"Yes," Jesse replied. "And it was so strange. It said something about searching the realm of the stars to learn. And then it asked me to come with it. But I refused."

"Good thinking, son," Coleman said, glowering. "You might have ended up like Gaines and Palmer!"

"It must have been checking us out, to see how well we're armed. Don't you think, Colonel?" Alex asked Coleman.

"Sure. It was looking for our soft spot—the observatory," the colonel said. "It's the only building above ground—and the one most easily attacked." His voice clearly indicated he was in battle mode. "Osgood, come with me. We need to check all exits again. Make sure everything is secure."

After they left, Jesse stood looking out through the observatory dome. A spot of pink lit up the sky for a moment. Suddenly, he realized that the light was being reflected off something. He saw it then, something gold lying outside the observatory, something the creature had obviously left behind.

9

Without telling anyone, Jesse slipped into his space gear and headed outside. When he stooped to pick up the object, he could hardly believe his eyes. He carried it to his apartment where he continued to examine it.

It was tarnished, and he couldn't see everything extremely clearly. But he could see enough to recognize what it was.

It was a gold plaque about six by nine inches. The plaque featured a map of the solar system, a drawing of a spacecraft, and the picture of a man and woman. The man's hand was raised in greeting.

Now, at last, Jesse understood the creature's strange gesture. It had been trying to imitate what the man on the plaque was doing. The creature was trying to tell Jesse that, like the man on the plaque, it, too, was friendly.

But if it was friendly, why had it taken Elliott Gaines and Robin Palmer? Jesse wondered.

Jesse couldn't sleep much that night. He caught ten minutes here and there, but he kept waking up. If the settlement was going into a war mode, Jesse either had to get through to the colonists or to those creatures before violence broke out.

But Jesse doubted that he could get through to Colonel Coleman or even to Dr. Chin anymore. The two men felt threatened by the bird creatures and would do whatever it took to garrison the settlement. He decided to talk to Lara Soto about it. He got up early and took a chance at knocking on her door. He hoped she was awake.

Like Jesse, Dr. Soto had spent a sleepless night. Without hesitation, she invited him in to share a cup of hot, black coffee.

"Lara, last night one of the creatures came to the observatory window and talked to me," Jesse said.

"Talked to you?" Lara said, surprised. "You mean it speaks English?"

"I think it uses a translator device to speak," Jesse explained.

"What did it say?" Lara wanted to know.

"Something about searching the realm of the stars for knowledge," Jesse replied. "Anyway, it left something behind."

He laid the gold plaque on the table between them. "These were put into space probes back in the 1970s," Jesse began. "The probes were sent deep into space in the hopes that if aliens found them, they would know about us and realize that we are a peaceful race. Lara, this creature raised its hand in greeting just like the guy on the plaque, see?"

Lara's eyes flashed with anger. "What about Elliott and Robin? What did those monsters do with them?"

"I asked the creature, and it said, 'Come with me,' " Jesse said.

"Come with it? So it could destroy you too?" Lara asked bitterly.

"I don't know, Lara, but I have a feeling that they mean no harm," Jesse said. "I could be wrong, but I think it's just a coincidence that they are exploring Mars at the same time we are. If they did take Elliott and Robin, maybe they just wanted to talk to them and just haven't sent them back yet."

"So you think there's a chance Elliott is still alive?" Lara asked, excitement building in her voice.

"My gut feeling is that he is," Jesse replied. "I don't think those creatures mean to harm anyone."

****

In the morning Colonel Coleman called a meeting of all the colonists. He had maps on the wall, and he stood with a pointer ready to describe the defense strategy. A sullen Dr. Chin sat on the sidelines. He might still be the commander, but it was in name only. Coleman had taken over. The whole thrust of the MEC II program had changed overnight. From a scientific project it had become a desperate effort to fight off alien invaders and stay alive.

"By now, all of you have received some training in firearms," the colonel began. "We're in the process of developing a plan of defense, and every man and woman must be ready to blast away if the creatures attack."

"I want to say something," Jesse

interrupted. He reminded them about the plaques from the *Pioneer* program. He said he found one of the plaques where the creature had spoken to him. "I think this creature found the plaque and was using it to tell me that they did not want trouble. It raised its hand in greeting, just like the man on the plaque."

"Nonsense," Coleman said in his booming voice. "They would not have kidnapped our people if they were a peaceful race. Don't give us this sentimental nonsense, Garcia. Make no mistake—we are facing the fight of our lives!"

"I think Colonel Coleman is right," Alex Osgood said. "They don't want us here, and they will use every strategy they can to get rid of us. The creature who spoke to you, Jesse, wanted to lull you into a false sense of security. We've got to have weapons ready and blast these feathered friends from the sky when they show their faces around here. Get them before they get us."

"Jesse brought up the idea that Elliott and Robin could still be alive," Dr. Soto said. "*If* the creatures are friendly, surely an unprovoked attack on them would endanger our friends' lives."

"Dr. Soto, I'm sorry to have to say this, but in my opinion, Gaines and Palmer are dead," the colonel said. "If they weren't, we'd have seen them by now. As the military specialist, I say we hit the creatures the minute we see them approach the settlement. As Osgood said, get them before they get any more of us. Besides, you're the one who's said all along that they don't want us here."

"Not wanting us here and wanting to harm us are two different things, Colonel," Lara pointed out. "I just think we should keep an open mind about this. Maybe they're hostile and maybe not. But wouldn't it be terrible if we started a war when we didn't have to? Dr. Chin, what do you think? Surely you agree with me."

Dr. Chin was silent a moment before answering. Finally, he said, "I think we need to take steps to ensure that no more crew members are lost. I agree with Coleman and Osgood. It's better to strike them first if we get the chance. We don't know what those creatures are capable of."

"All right, you heard the commander," Colonel Coleman said. "Here's the list of assignments. Listen up!"

Jesse sighed as the colonel read off the assignments. As he had feared, getting through to Chin or Coleman was impossible. Jesse wasn't even sure of his own theory. Maybe it was just wishful thinking on his part. Maybe the creatures *did* mean them harm. Then again, maybe they didn't. And it saddened him to see that everyone was so sure that violence was the only course of action.

10

Preparations to defend the settlement began. Everyone received an assignment and a high-powered firearm. The exits were reinforced, and guards were posted 24 hours a day.

Toward evening on the third day, as the moon began to sink below the horizon, everyone heard a muted roar in the distance. They rushed to the observatory to search the sky.

"Here they come!" Colonel Coleman shouted.

A great globelike object seemed to almost fill the darkening Martian sky. It glowed with lights as it hovered over the MEC II settlement.

"Look at that," one of the colonists groaned. "It looks like they're positioning themselves to bomb us!"

"We're doomed," another cried. "Our flimsy buildings aren't resistant to heavy explosives, even though the buildings are underground."

"Everyone to your station!" Colonel Coleman bellowed. "Prepare to attack—and be attacked!"

"Wait, it's not bombing us! It's landing!" Jesse said. He turned to Dr. Chin. "Dr. Chin, please. Wait until we see what the creatures are doing here. If they wanted to kill us, they could have dropped something on us from above. I think they want to communicate."

"Please, Dr. Chin. Jesse may be right," Lara Soto said. "They're not firing on us."

Through the clear dome, Dr. Chin watched the ship slowly descend.

"All right," he said. "Colonel Coleman, hold on a minute."

"But—" Coleman protested.

"I'm still commander of this colony," Dr. Chin declared with surprising authority. "Hold your fire until I give the go-ahead."

The large ship came closer to the red earth. Like a helicopter, it kicked up dust, creating a small pink dust storm underneath its belly.

Finally, it settled down lightly on the Martian soil.

Everyone watched, waiting for hordes of bird creatures to come streaming out, armed with weapons nobody had ever seen before. For a few minutes nothing happened. Everyone seemed to be holding his or her breath. Everyone except Colonel Coleman.

"It'll be like the story of the Trojan Horse," Coleman warned. "The Greeks gave the horse to the Trojans as a gift. But when they wheeled the huge horse up to the gates of the city, Greek soldiers climbed out of it and destroyed Troy. Just wait till those winged monsters come crawling out of that ship!"

"We don't know that for sure, sir," Jesse said.

Suddenly, a huge opening appeared in the side of the ship. It was high up on the gleaming silver body.

"Look, there's something in the doorway!" Alex cried.

"What in the—" Colonel Coleman exclaimed. "It's got a space suit on—just like ours!"

Jesse blinked. The colonel was right. Whatever was standing in that doorway had on a space suit from Earth. Jesse watched as one of the winged creatures came up alongside the space-suited one.

"Good Lord! Look at that thing!" Rebecca Newhall said, her eyes wide with awe.

Suddenly, the winged creature picked up the space-suited one and flew to the ground. There it gently set the space-suited figure down. Immediately, the figure came bounding toward the settlement.

"Prepare to fire!" the colonel yelled.

"No, wait!" Lara Soto cried. "It's Elliott! And there's Robin in the doorway!"

A gasp went up from the colonists as Robin Palmer was assisted out of the spaceship by another winged creature. Once on the ground, Robin headed toward the settlement. The winged creatures returned to their ship. When the creatures reached the doorway, they turned around and raised their right hands to the colonists. Then the door slid shut, disappearing once more into the wall of the great ship. A few seconds later, the ship was high in the Martian sky. It was visible for a long time until at last it appeared as no more than a bright disk, merging with the stars.

The colonists joyously welcomed Elliott Gaines and Robin Palmer back. In the observatory, the two explorers told their stories.

"One of them approached me as I was walking to the Rover," Elliott said. "It picked me up in its arms and then flew me to its ship."

"How did they treat you?" Colonel Coleman wanted to know.

"They treated me kindly," Elliott replied. "They were curious about where I came from. I told them we came from Earth and that we came in peace."

"How about you, Palmer? How did they treat you?" the colonel asked.

Robin Palmer said, "The same. They never once threatened me. They were simply curious about us—what our mission was and how long we intended to be here. They thought at first that we were not intelligent life because we were so different from them. And they were a little worried because they feared an attack from the settlement."

"They have no weapons," Elliott said. "They came completely unarmed."

"They were camped on Phobos for a while. Then they came to explore Mars itself," Robin said. "Like us, they're looking for a planet to colonize. But they found this one unsuitable."

"No trees?" Alex asked, smiling.

Everyone chuckled at Alex's joke.

"Actually, they're looking for a certain type of red soil, but this isn't it," Elliott said.

"So they're gone—for good?" Colonel Coleman asked. Jesse noticed that the older man looked somewhat disappointed.

"Yes," Elliott said. "They finished their mission here and are moving on to explore another planet."

Dr. Chin smiled and clasped his hands, "Then we can proceed with MEC II!" he said. "None of us has to leave!"

A cheer arose from the small crowd. Jesse saw Elliott Gaines place his arm around Lara Soto's shoulders. Both were smiling dreamily, once again picturing skyscrapers and parks and families leading happy existences on Mars.

Jesse looked at Bianca. She smiled and said, "Looks like we're stuck together for a year or so. Think you can stand it?"

"Suits me just fine!" Jesse replied. He placed his arm around her as they watched Phobos set—for the third time that day.